THE SIEGE OF EARTH III

Dominick Tobin

POOLBEG

Published in 1995
by Poolbeg Press Ltd
123 Baldoyle Industrial Estate
Dublin 13, Ireland

© Dominick Tobin 1995

The moral right of the author has been asserted.

A catalogue record for this book is available from the British Library.

ISBN 1 85371 482 8

Cover illustration by Jane Doran
Cover design by Poolbeg Group Services Ltd
Set by Poolbeg Group Services Ltd in Palatino
Printed by The Guernsey Press Ltd,
Vale, Guernsey, Channel Islands.

*For the Ballincurry Timothys; Vera,
Mary Kate (Deceased), Owen, Mike, Christy,
my namesake Domnick (Deceased) and especially
my mother Brigid.*

A Secret Level

Tim's mother's head appeared at the bedroom door.

"Time for bed now, Tim," she said. "It's getting late."

The thin brown-haired boy, who was sitting in front of a screen, turned on his swivel-chair to face his mother.

"I just want to try this game again," he said.

"It's too late," insisted his mother. "You won't be able to get up for school in the morning."

"Please, Mum," pleaded Tim, "it'll only take a few minutes, and look, I'm already in my pyjamas."

He jumped up so that his mother could see that he was wearing his sky-blue pyjamas.

"Oh, all right," agreed his mother reluctantly, "but only until you finish one more game. Remember, even twelve-year-old boys need their sleep."

"Thanks, Mum," said Tim. He sat back down on the chair and swivelled around to face the screen again.

Getting this old television was the best thing that ever happened, decided Tim. Now I can play my games without disturbing Mum and Dad.

He pressed the "Start" key and waited for the game to come up on screen.

I always get to at least level five, he thought, but tonight I can't even get past level two. It's very strange.

He drummed his fingers on the table while he waited impatiently for the game to appear, then pressed the "Start" key again. The screen suddenly went completely blank, flashed and then lit up again.

A small white object appeared on the left side of the screen.

That's strange, thought Tim, that shouldn't be there. I must have pressed the wrong key.

He reached over to the small computer beside the television and pressed the "Reset" key to clear the screen. The computer bleeped loudly, but the strange object didn't move.

On the right side of the screen another strange object appeared. This time it was square with the word "BASE" written on it.

With the back of his hand, Tim brushed his hair away from his eyes. He had a puzzled look on his face and he stared hard at the screen.

What's going on? he wondered.

Once more he pressed the "Reset" key. Again the computer bleeped loudly, but still the screen didn't clear.

It must be some kind of secret level . . . but how did it get on my computer? Tim wondered.

He flicked the joy-stick back and forth. The white object moved accordingly.

When he depressed the button at the top of the joy-stick, a thin broken line shot from the front of the white object and exploded halfway across the screen.

It's some kind of fighter, Tim decided, but what am I supposed to do with it?

As if by way of an answer, six black objects appeared between the white fighter and "BASE".

"So you want to play," said Tim to himself.

He moved the joy-stick to the right and the white fighter moved across the screen. At the same time the six black fighters moved to meet him.

Tim pressed the firing button. A line of fire shot from the front of his fighter but exploded short of the black fighters.

I must be out of range, he decided.

Suddenly, the black fighters opened fire. Explosions flashed around Tim's fighter and only his quick and expert manoeuvring saved the fighter from being blow off the screen.

They're out of my range, but I'm in their range, thought Tim. This is going to be difficult.

The black fighters were now bearing down on the white one. Two of them stayed in the centre of the screen, while two went to the left and the other two went to the right.

They're trying to surround me, observed Tim. Let's see how they like a backward loop . . .

He pushed the joy-stick forward and the white fighter climbed quickly and steeply. A quick flick of his wrist flipped the fighter into a backward loop. As it came up out of the loop, a black fighter drifted into Tim's path.

Tim pressed the firing button.

"Got him!" he shouted, as a flash on the screen indicated a hit.

Another black fighter drifted across Tim's path. Once more, Tim pressed the firing button. Again, a flash on the screen showed the fighter had been destroyed.

By now the black fighters' formation was in disarray, and Tim was already on the tail of two more of them. His thumb hovered above the firing button before he finally pressed it. Once, twice. Two bursts of fire shot from the front of the fighter. Two more flashes appeared on the screen to indicate two more direct hits.

The remaining two black fighters had now regrouped and they were charging full speed at Tim's fighter. Their guns blazed as explosions flashed around the white fighter.

"It's time I got out of here," whispered Tim under his breath.

He pushed the joy-stick to the left, then flicked it back and forth as he set a zigzag course towards the bottom of the screen.

Still the black fighters pursued him at speed. All the time their guns blazed.

The bottom of the screen was getting closer and closer. The black fighters were getting closer and closer. Explosions flashed all around him, but still Tim kept on course.

He had almost reached the bottom of the screen. The white fighter was about to crash.

Suddenly Tim pushed the joy-stick to the left. His fighter responded instantly.

The black fighters were taken by surprise by Tim's sudden movement and couldn't react quickly enough. Two flashes at the bottom of the screen indicated that they had crashed.

Tim smiled with satisfaction.

"That's them finished," he said to himself.

He pushed the joy-stick to the right and up slightly. The fighter inched its way across the screen until it docked safely at "BASE".

Suddenly the screen went blank.

What's going on? wondered Tim as he looked at the blank screen. Where's my score?

The screen flashed, then flashed again and again.

A small bright dot appeared in the centre of the screen. For a few moments it didn't move, then very slowly it began to rotate in small circles.

Gradually the dot began to pick up speed. It spun faster and faster and the circles got wider and wider.

This is weird, thought Tim.

He pressed the "Reset" key, but nothing happened.

The dot kept spinning faster and faster. Soon it was whirling around the screen at tremendous speed in ever-increasing circles.

Tim depressed the "Eject" button and the cartridge jumped from his computer, but the dot kept spinning. He pressed the "Off" button, but it had no effect. He pressed it again and again and again, but nothing happened. It was as if the computer had a mind of its own.

He reached across and flicked off the main power switch, but even that made no difference.

By now the screen was full of swirling circles. Tim

began to panic. Something had taken control of his computer!

He reached down to pull the plug from its socket, but his hand never reached the socket.

His gaze was drawn to the dot in the centre of the circles. He couldn't look away. The swirling circles had him hypnotised. He tried to move his arms and legs, but they seemed to be frozen by the circles of light which had jumped from the screen and were flashing all around him. He was caught like a fly in a spider's web.

Suddenly he was lifted from his chair. The screen loomed up in front of him as if he had been shrunk to a fraction of his normal size. The bright dot had now become a door at the top of a long dark corridor.

"Help!" screamed Tim, as he was sucked towards the centre of the screen.

A Parallel Galaxy

The grip of the swirling circles got tighter and tighter. Tim could feel himself being pulled down the corridor at tremendous speed. And all the time a constant high-pitched zinging noise rang in his head.

Tim closed his eyes.

This can't be happening to me, he thought.

Gradually the circles loosened their grip, the pulling eased and the zinging noise died away. Soon all was quiet and still.

Slowly Tim opened one eye, then the other.

He was standing in what appeared to be a small glass cubicle, no bigger than a public phone box. Outside the cubicle, dressed in a green shirt and trousers, stood a blond-haired boy no older than himself.

The boy opened the door of the glass cubicle and Tim stepped out. He could now see that the cubicle was contained within a larger room, and was connected to the ceiling by what looked like electric cables.

Across the room was a control panel, with knobs and switches and small flashing lights of all kinds.

The blond-haired boy stood to attention.

"Welcome aboard, sir," he said. "My name is Uli, and I'm to take you to the Commander."

Tim looked around to see whom Uli had spoken to, but quickly realised that he had been talking to him.

"Where am I?" asked the confused Tim.

"The Commander will explain everything to you," replied Uli.

He led Tim out of the room and down a long corridor until they came to a door with the word "BRIDGE" written on it. There was a small control panel on the wall beside the door. Uli keyed in some numbers and the door slid silently open.

They were now in a large room which had two levels. Around the perimeter of the room, on the higher level, men sat at computer screens. They were all dressed in the same green-coloured uniform that Uli was wearing.

The centre of the room was the lower level. Here three men sat around a glass-topped table. Uli led Tim to these three men.

On the right sat a small fat man with a round red face. He wore a grey uniform with one stripe on each shoulder. On the left sat a thin man with octagonal glasses. He also wore a grey uniform with one stripe on each shoulder. Between the men in the grey uniforms sat a big stocky man with grey hair. He was wearing a dark blue uniform and had three stripes on each of his broad shoulders.

The two men in grey uniforms whispered to each other.

"He's very young," said the one with the round face.

"And his clothes are strange," added the thin man.

Tim's eyes flicked from one man to the other. He felt just as he had the time the Headmaster called him to his office for breaking a window with a football.

Finally the big man in the blue uniform spoke.

"Welcome aboard the Command Starship *Alpha I*," he said. "My name is Commander Ford. This is General Lee," the man with the round face smiled, "and this is General Yore." The man with the octagonal glasses nodded slightly to acknowledge his introduction.

"What should we call you?" asked General Lee.

"T . . . T . . . Tim, s . . . s . . . sir," stuttered Tim nervously. "Tim Timothy."

"Well, Captain Tim," continued Commander Ford, "I suppose you are wondering where you are and why we sent for you?"

"Y . . . Y . . . Yes sir" replied Tim, "I *was* wondering."

"You are in what's known as a parallel galaxy," began the Commander. "It is like when you look in a mirror, you see an image of yourself. The image is real and yet it's not, because it's not part of your world. We are like that image. We are part of the Earth Federation. Our *Earth I* is like a mirror image of your Earth, except that we are far more advanced. We are like what your Earth will be in a thousand years. You can see from the people in this room that we appear to be exactly like the humans on your Earth."

Tim looked around the room. What the Commander had said was true. He could have been in a control room on any ship or any aeroplane on Earth, but he wasn't.

"If I'm not on Earth, then where am I?" he asked in amazement.

Commander Ford pressed a button at the side of the table and the glass tabletop lit up in a chart.

A flashing dot, in the centre of other dots,

appeared at General Lee's end of the table. Another dot flashed in front of General Yore.

Commander Ford pointed to the flashing dot in front of General Lee.

"This is your Earth," he told Tim, "and these other dots are your solar system. Here is Venus, Pluto, Mars, Neptune . . . "

He pointed across the table to the flashing dot in front of General Yore.

"This is our *Earth I*," he said.

Tim looked from one flashing dot across the table to the other. It seemed like a very long way.

"How far apart are they?" he asked out of curiosity.

"If you were to travel from your Earth to our *Earth I* at full speed in your fastest space rocket, you would be thousands of years old by the time you arrived," said the Commander. "If you were to travel at the speed of your Sun's light, it would take about five of your years. And even then you might not find our galaxy.

"As I said, we are a parallel galaxy. We exist alongside other galaxies, but we cannot be seen through a telescope."

A parallel galaxy five light-years away, thought Tim. He found it hard to believe and wasn't convinced. He knew from his science class in school that light travelled at 186,000 miles per *second*, so five light years would be about 30 billion miles! How could he have travelled such a distance in just a few seconds?

"If I am so far away from Planet Earth, how did I get here so quickly?" he asked.

"You were transported," the Commander

answered matter-of-factly, as if it was an everyday occurrence.

Tim started to laugh nervously.

"There is no such thing as transportation," he began uneasily, "it only exists in comics."

General Yore gave him a long hard stare.

"Transportation may not exist in your world," he said coldly, "but I can assure you it is a reality here."

Tim fell silent. He stared at the floor and shifted uneasily. He felt like a fool.

"Most of the things you ever heard about space will mean nothing in our galaxy," said the Commander kindly.

"Although you didn't feel yourself shrinking, you were in fact shrunk to a single molecule. That enabled us to bring you here on a transportation beam. You were then returned to your normal size in the transportation cubicle."

Tim just stared at the Commander in bewilderment. He didn't know what to say. It all seemed so fantastic.

"There will be a lot of things that you will not understand," continued the Commander. "Do not try to understand them all – just accept them as they are."

"But why did you bring me here?" asked Tim.

Commander Ford folded his arms on top of the glass table and sighed. He had a serious look on his face.

"We're in trouble, Tim," he said slowly. "The Federation is under attack by a ruthless race known as the Rylons. They are trying to extend their Empire and have already taken over a number of small planets. At this moment they have *Earth III* under siege."

"What is *Earth III*?" asked Tim.

"*Earth III* is one of our inhabited satellites," explained the Commander.

He pressed another button at the side of the table. Once again the glass top lit up and a chart appeared.

This time the chart was divided into ten sections. In the first section, at the top left hand corner of the table, there was a large dot. Close to this dot was a smaller flashing dot. There was a similar large dot in the bottom right hand corner in section ten. Two smaller dots, one in section four and another in section seven, also appeared on the chart.

"This is the Third Quadrant of our Solar System," explained Commander Ford. "Each of the sections is called a Cemirand. The large dot in Cemirand One is *Earth I*, and the flashing dot beside it is this ship, the *Alpha I*. The large dot in Cemirand Ten is *Earth III*. The two smaller dots represent spacestations. *Space Station I*, in Cemirand Four, is a supply depot, while *Space Station II* in Cemirand Seven is a refuelling depot."

The Commander took a deep breath and folded his arms again.

"*Earth III* was discovered 150 years ago, by our great explorer, Marco Colo. It was a dead star until we colonised it twenty years ago. There are now five million people living on it.

"Unfortunately, the water on *Earth III* is poisonous and they need purification crystals to make it drinkable. When we last heard from them, they had barely enough fresh water left to last them three days.

"If we can't break the Rylon blockade, and get the crystals to them, the people will either die or have to surrender to the Rylons. If they surrender, many will be murdered, and those who aren't murdered will be forced to work as slaves for the Rylons.

"Even worse, if *Earth III* falls to the Rylons there is nothing to stop them attacking *Earth I*, and then 200 million people will be in danger.

"So you see, Tim, we must stop the Rylons."

"I can see that," said Tim, "but I still don't understand why I'm here."

"The Rylon fighters are faster and more powerful than ours," explained the Commander. "We have been engaged in battle with them on many occasions and each time our fighters have been defeated. Our fighter squadrons are now both depleted and disheartened. What we need is a fighter pilot of outstanding ability. Someone who, despite the disadvantages of having a slower fighter and less fire-power, can take on the Rylons and defeat them. Now at last we have found that person." The Commander and the two Generals looked at Tim.

He could hardly believe his ears. He would have been flattered, only he was too shocked.

"W . . . W . . . What makes you think that I'm that person?" he stammered.

"That game you played on your computer was not just an ordinary video game," said Commander Ford. "It was a fighter pilot test. It was put on thousands of computers all over your Earth – you were the only one to succeed. We are somewhat surprised that you are so young but, nevertheless, you are the best. You are the only one that can help us – we need you."

Before Tim had a chance to speak, a man at one of the computer screens suddenly swung round. He seemed very agitated.

"We've lost communications with *Space Station I*, Commander," he shouted.

"Can we bring it up on screen?" asked the Commander.

"No, sir," replied the man. "We are still outside visual range."

Commander Ford stared silently at the glass table. When he spoke again, he spoke quietly, as if thinking out loud.

"It might just be a simple communications failure," he said, "or it might be the Rylons."

He looked up at Tim.

"Will you help us?" he asked.

Tim thought for a moment before answering. It was a big responsibility, but surely they wouldn't have chosen him unless they thought he could help.

"I'll help you," he agreed.

The three men behind the glass-topped table smiled. Even General Yore looked pleased.

"Thank you," said Commander Ford. "Uli will get your uniform and show you the way to the fighter hangar. Your first assignment will be to see what has happened to *Space Station I*. Just one more thing. Take no chances with the Rylons. They don't follow the same moral code as you and I," explained the Commander. "They have no conscience. They look on respect and concern for other living beings as a form of weakness. Keep all such thoughts out of your mind. Remember, they have slaughtered thousands of people and will slaughter thousands more if they are given the chance. They must be stopped. Good luck, Captain Tim."

First Assignment

Uli led Tim back down the corridor until they came to another door.

Once again he keyed in a code and the door slid open.

"There are the pilots' quarters," explained Uli.

On the right, as they went in, there was a dormitory and on the left a changing-room. Uli brought Tim into the changing-room.

"The pilots are resting," he said. "They are on constant stand-by."

He handed Tim a one-piece flying suit with a zip up the middle and a pair of canvas shoes.

"You can put this on over the clothes you're wearing," he said.

It's the same colour as my pyjamas, thought Tim, as he looked at the light blue uniform.

"Your utility knife is in the pocket," said Uli. "It has many functions, it can be used as a knife, a screwdriver, a scissors, or even a torch. You may find it handy."

As Tim climbed into the flying suit, he felt the cold steel of the knife in his right hip-pocket.

At the neck of the suit there was a small microphone.

"That is your communicator, for when you are not in your fighter," explained Uli. "Just press the button on the collar when you want to speak. Now follow me and I will show you the way to the fighter hangar."

At the end of the hall there was a circular room, with a shiny silver pole running down from the ceiling through a gap in the floor to a lower level.

It's just like a fireman's pole, thought Tim.

They slid down the pole to an area like an underground carpark. Silver fighters were parked in bays on both sides of the hangar.

On one side, the fighters had a red disc at the front and were numbered from one to six. On the other side, the fighters had a green disc in the same place. These were also numbered from one to six.

Uli showed Tim to a light-blue-coloured fighter which was almost the same colour as his flying suit.

"This is your fighter," he told Tim.

The fighter was about the same size as a car, except it had no doors. The cockpit was completely glass, and slid back to allow the pilot to climb in. At the back of the fighter there were two big jets while, at the front, a small oblong opening beneath the cockpit housed the twin cannons.

"How will I know how to fly it?" asked Tim.

"The fighter is computerised," said Uli. "The computer will explain everything to you."

Uli pulled open the cockpit and Tim climbed in. When he was seated comfortably in the single seat, Uli closed the cockpit and gave him the thumbs-up sign.

The cockpit was small and everything was close at hand.

In front of Tim there was a two-handled control, with a button on the top of the handle on the right. Set between the handles were the circular sights. Behind the control there was an instrument panel, with clocks and gauges and a small blank screen.

"Please identify yourself," demanded a monotonous mechanical voice that startled Tim.

"Who are you? Where are you?" he asked, as he glanced nervously around the cockpit.

"Please identify yourself," demanded the voice again.

This time, Tim could see it came from a small speaker on the instrument panel.

"My name is Captain Tim Timothy," said Tim proudly. He still wasn't used to the "Captain" title, but he thought it had a nice ring to it.

"Welcome aboard, Captain Tim," said the voice. "I am the Computerised Automation System model 435798B, but you can call me CAS."

"Thank you, CAS," said Tim. "Please tell me what you can do?"

CAS seemed to be annoyed by Tim's question.

"I can fly and navigate, I can operate the radar and laser cannons, I can calculate distances and speed, I can operate the sonic scanner and open communications channels. In fact, I can do almost everything," it answered indignantly.

"Can you score a goal from twenty-five yards?" asked Tim jokingly.

"The word 'goal' is not contained in my memory banks. Please explain," said CAS.

"Never mind," said Tim. "It was only a joke."

"The word 'joke' is not contained in my memory banks," said CAS again. "Please explain."

Just what I need, thought Tim. A computer without a sense of humour.

"How do I operate you?" he asked.

"I react to verbal commands from a recognised source," said CAS. "Your voice pattern has been locked into my memory."

"Are there any manual controls?" asked Tim.

"The control handles in front of you will steer the fighter and operate the laser cannons," explained CAS. "If you push the right handle, the fighter will turn right. If you push the left handle, the fighter will turn left. If you push both handles together the fighter will descend, and if you pull back both handles together the fighter will climb. The right handle rotates to direct the cannons, and the target shows up in the sights in front of you. The button on top of the right handle fires the cannons.

"However, I must advise you that I am far more efficient and effective than any pilot using the manual controls."

A computer with a big head and no sense of humour, thought Tim. Just my luck.

"OK, CAS, let's roll," he said. "Destination *Space Station I*."

The fighter moved smoothly out of the bay, turned right and glided across the floor. The hangar doors slid open and the fighter slipped out into the blackness of space.

In the cockpit, the instrument panel threw a faint

light, but outside it was complete blackness. Tim had never experienced such darkness. It was even darker than the night the electricity went off during the bad storm the previous winter.

"What do I have to do?" asked Tim.

"You need do nothing," replied CAS. "The co-ordinates of our destination and the flight path have been locked in."

"Let's go then," said Tim as he pulled across the seat belt and clicked it into its receiver.

The engines fired to life and the fighter blasted off. The incredible acceleration caught Tim by surprise and he was flung back against the seat.

When he got over the sudden jolt, he found it hard to know if the fighter was moving at all. There was nothing outside in the blackness to show that it was moving. It was like that strange sensation in a lift. A jerk to start, then nothing, until another jerk and suddenly you're six stories up.

"What speed are we doing?" he asked CAS.

"We are travelling at twenty five kilomiles per demihour," CAS informed him.

"Is that fast?" asked Tim.

"It is 50,000 of your Earth miles every hour," said CAS.

"That is fast," agreed Tim. "How far is it to *Space Station I*?"

"*Space Station I* is located in Demirand Four. Total distance from our present position is six kilomiles," recited CAS.

There was silence for a few seconds, then CAS came to life once more.

"It will take us exactly seven of your minutes and twelve of your seconds to reach our destination," it added, before Tim had a chance to calculate.

CAS went quiet. Tim looked out through the cockpit glass, but there was nothing to see.

Five minutes later, CAS came to life again.

"We are now within radar and communication range of *Space Station I*," it announced.

Tim glanced at the radar hand sweep around the screen. There was no "bleep" to indicate the existence of *Space Station* I.

"*Space Station I* is not replying to our communications," said CAS. "Radar shows that it is no longer in its last known position."

"How long until we reach that position?" asked Tim.

"Twenty-seven of your seconds," calculated CAS.

A sudden jerk, exactly twenty-seven seconds later, told Tim that they had stopped. CAS confirmed it.

"We are now in the last known position of *Space Station I*," it said.

Through the cockpit glass, Tim could see small bits of shiny metal debris floating in space.

"Is that all that's left of *Space Station I*?" he wondered.

"I have scanned the metal debris," said CAS. "The conformation and density is the same as the metal used in *Space Station I*."

"That's that, then," said Tim with a sigh. "Contact the Command ship."

"We are outside communications range," said CAS.

"Contact with Command Starship *Alpha I* is not possible."

Bleep, bleep, bleep . . . bleep, bleep, bleep. Suddenly the radar bleeped six times.

"Six spacecraft approaching at speed," announced CAS.

"What are they?" asked Tim.

"My scanner identifies them as Rylon fighters," replied CAS.

Well, I won't be able to outrun them, thought Tim, so it looks like I'm going to find out just how good these Rylons are.

Battle with the Rylons

"OK, CAS, let's see what this thing can do," said Tim. "Switch to manual control."

"Automatic system has now been disengaged," confirmed CAS. "I should warn you that the range of the Rylon laser cannons is .2 kilomiles, while the range of our laser cannons is only .1 kilomiles."

That does give them an advantage, thought Tim.

He held the control handles tightly and moved them slightly backwards and forwards. The fighter responded smoothly. In the distance he could see a row of six faint lights.

"How long before we're within Rylon range?" asked Tim.

"Ten seconds," replied CAS.

Suddenly the Rylons broke their line. Two Rylons went to Tim's left and two more to his right.

They're trying to surround me, just like in the game, thought Tim. I wonder how they'll enjoy a backward loop?

"Five seconds until we are within Rylon laser range," warned CAS.

Tim held his course steady. The lights of the Rylon

fighters were getting brighter and brighter as they closed in.

"Rylon lasers are now locked in," said CAS. "Three seconds until we are within their range."

Still Tim held his course.

"Two seconds . . . one second . . . "

Tim pulled hard on the controls and the fighter banked steeply.

There was a "hiss" as the Rylon lasers flashed below the fighter.

Tim continued to pull hard on the controls. The fighter drifted up and back, until it had flipped into a backward loop.

Luckily for Tim, his fighter could turn quicker and tighter than the Rylons, and as he came up out of his loop he was behind them. Now, instead of being the hunted, he was the hunter.

He twisted the right control handle until a Rylon came into his sights.

"Lock lasers," he commanded.

"Lasers locked," confirmed CAS.

"Fire," he ordered.

For a second Tim hesitated. It was one thing shooting down fighters in video games, it was a different thing in reality. Then he remembered the Commander's words. *Take no chances . . . no conscience . . . slaughtered thousands . . .*

There was a blinding flash of light as the Rylon exploded in a ball of flames.

"Attention," warned CAS. "The four other Rylon fighters are closing in."

Tim glanced out through the cockpit glass. He

could see the lights of the Rylon fighters bearing down on him, but they were too late to save their comrade. Tim already had him in his sights.

"Lock lasers," he commanded again.

"Lasers locked," replied CAS.

"Fire."

Once again the Rylon disappeared in an explosive flash.

The other Rylon fighters were almost on top of Tim now. His fighter rocked and shook, as a barrage of Rylon laser fire exploded around him.

"It's time I got out of here," he said to himself.

Tim pushed the control handles in as far as they would go. The fighter responded immediately, diving down . . .

CAS monitored the reaction of the Rylons on the Radar.

"Two Rylon fighters are in pursuit," it said. "The other two have fallen back to prevent you from looping."

"Good," said Tim. He eased back on the controls and gently moved the right and left handles alternately to set the fighter on a long, sweeping zigzag course.

"Tell me when the Rylons lock in their lasers," he told CAS.

"Rylon lasers locked in," confirmed CAS a few seconds later.

"Cut engines. Now!" shouted Tim.

There was a sudden jolt, as the fighter came to an immediate halt. The two pursuing Rylons were taken by surprise by Tim's sudden stop, and shot past him before they had time to react.

"Full speed forward," roared Tim.

There was another jerk, as the engines fired to life again.

Tim manoeuvred the right control until one of the Rylons came into his sights.

"Lock lasers and fire," he ordered.

A constant stream of laser fire spat from Tim's cannons and bombarded the Rylon. A thin line of smoke drifted from the back of the Rylon before it disappeared in a blinding flash.

"What are the other Rylons doing?" Tim asked CAS.

"They are still in the same position," CAS told him. "They appear to be stationery."

Why don't they help their comrade? wondered Tim. What are they waiting for?

The final Rylon fighter of the attacking group was now desperately trying to lose Tim. It turned this way and that in an attempt to avoid him, but it was no use. Tim was firmly on its tail. He adjusted the right control handle until the dark shape of the Rylon was fully in his sights.

"Lock and fire," he commanded.

There was a volley of laser fire from Tim's cannons. Pieces of the Rylon fighter were flung in hundreds of different directions as it exploded in one big blast.

"Now for those two cowards," decided Tim.

Bleep, bleep, bleep . . . bleep, bleep, bleep. Once again the radar hammered out a warning.

"What's going on?" demanded Tim.

"My scanner shows that six more Rylon fighters are approaching," said CAS.

So that's why the other two Rylons didn't attack, thought Tim. They were waiting for reinforcements.

"It's time to get out of here," he decided. "Eight Rylons are too many to take on. Set course to Command ship."

"Course to Command Starship *Alpha I* has been set," confirmed CAS. "However, Rylons are in pursuit."

"Contact the Command ship and tell them we need help," said Tim.

"We are still outside communications range," said CAS. "We cannot communicate for another four minutes and forty-two seconds. I should also point out that our laser cannon bank is almost exhausted, and we will be within Rylon laser range in one minute and twenty-seven seconds."

"What do you suggest I do?" asked Tim in desperation.

"I am a computer," replied CAS. "I do not make suggestions. I give the facts and carry out commands."

Well, that's just great, thought Tim sarcastically. Here I am stuck somewhere in space, light years from home, with nobody to help me and with eight alien fighters trying to blow me out of existence.

"One minute before we are in Rylon range," warned CAS.

The Asteroid Field

"Forty-five seconds until we are within Rylon cannon range," announced CAS.

"How long until we can contact the Command ship?" asked Tim.

"Three minutes and two seconds," calculated CAS.

Tim stared at the radar screen. He hoped to see a telltale bleep that would show that the Command ship was on its way, but all he saw were the eight bleeps of the pursuing Rylons.

Suddenly at the top of the screen, he noticed a slight crackle. He watched carefully as the radar hand swept round again. Yes, there it was. Not a bleep, but a definite crackle.

"What's causing that interference?" he asked CAS.

There was a pause of a second or two before CAS replied.

"My scanners identify it as a positively-charged asteroid field," it said.

"What exactly is that?" asked Tim.

"The asteroids are hard matter particles," replied CAS. "They appear to be held together in this field by some form of weak gravity, although they are constantly moving within the field. There is also a positive charge bouncing randomly between the asteroids."

"What are hard matter particles?" asked Tim.

"They are what you would call rocks," said CAS. "It is difficult to calculate their mass, but I would estimate that most are larger than this craft."

"Is it safe to pass through the field?" Tim asked.

"We are a negatively-charged craft," CAS told him. "It is safe to cross so long as the charge remains positive and providing we don't crash into the asteroids."

"Set course for asteroid field," ordered Tim.

"Course set," confirmed CAS. "We will be entering the asteroid field in precisely thirty-two seconds. We will be in Rylon laser range in twenty seconds."

That's twelve seconds when I'll have to avoid them, thought Tim.

He glanced behind. The lights of the Rylons were closing in quickly.

"Ten seconds to Rylon laser range," announced CAS.

Far in the distance, Tim could see a dull green glow. That must be the asteroid field, he decided.

"Five seconds until Rylon range," warned CAS.

Tim held the controls firmly in his hands. His stomach churned. He couldn't remember when he had last felt so scared.

"Rylon lasers have locked in," CAS informed him. "Three seconds . . . two seconds . . . one second . . . "

Tim pushed both controls and the fighter dived. A

barrage of Rylon laser fire hissed by his fighter and exploded around it.

"Rylon lasers locked in again," announced CAS.

Tim eased back on the controls and then pushed the left one. He swerved, just as a stream of laser fire streaked past. The fighter shuddered and shook, from the impact of a laser exploding nearby.

Suddenly Tim was flung violently forward. The seat belt restricted his propulsion, but even still his head bumped against the cockpit glass before he fell back into his seat again.

"What happened – were we hit?" he asked in panic, as he rubbed his sore head.

"There is no damage to our craft," replied CAS. "The severe vibration was the result of a blast close to our port side. Rylon lasers have locked in again."

Tim could almost feel the Rylons closing in on him. Any second now they would press the firing button and his fighter would be blown to smithereens.

Suddenly his mind was taken off the Rylons as the fighter was enveloped by the dull green gloom of the asteroid field.

Tim blinked twice to get his eyes used to the strange green colour. And just in time. Out of the gloom, an asteroid hurtled straight at his fighter. He swung on the controls and the fighter swerved. The asteroid whirled by, just missing the fighter by inches.

A bright red flash in the green of the asteroid field told Tim that one of the pursuing Rylons had not been so lucky.

He glanced at the radar. The screen was blank.

"What's wrong with the radar?" he asked CAS.

"Due to the closeness of the asteroids and the presence of the positive charge, the radar is not operational," CAS told him. "However the last reading before we entered the asteroid field showed that six Rylons were pursuing us, while two had changed course and appear to be trying to circumnavigate the field."

Another asteroid appeared out of the gloom, followed by another. Tim pushed the right control and then the left. The fighter zigzagged between the asteroids.

By now, Tim's eyes had got used to the green gloom. The asteroids were acting as a barrier between him and the Rylons, so for the moment he was safe from them. All he had to worry about was avoiding the asteroids.

A large asteroid suddenly charged at him. Tim pushed both controls. The fighter dived, but straight into the path of three oncoming asteroids.

"Reduce speed," roared Tim.

There was a slight jerk as the fighter slowed down. Tim pushed the right control to avoid the first asteroid, then the left control to avoid the next, and then the right control again.

He sighed with relief.

"Phew! That was close," he said.

There was a bright flash behind, followed quickly by another flash, as two of the pursuing Rylons collided with the asteroids.

Tim smiled.

"That's two less to worry about," he said to himself.

Suddenly the asteroid field changed to a deep orange colour.

"What's happening, CAS?" demanded Tim.

"The presence of the fighters in the field has made it unstable," explained CAS. "The charge has changed from a positive charge to a neutral charge. We have fifteen seconds to get clear of the field before it changes to a negative charge."

"What will happen when it changes?" asked Tim.

"If two negative charges come together, it results in instant combustion," said CAS.

"You mean we'll burn up," said Tim.

"That is correct," agreed CAS.

"Return to full speed," commanded Tim.

Another asteroid appeared out of the gloom and streaked angrily towards them. Just in time, Tim pushed the right control and the fighter swerved to safety out of its deadly path.

"What's the quickest way out of this field?" asked Tim.

"My scanners are unable to operate," said CAS, "but we have been travelling now for thirty-five seconds through the field."

That rules turning back out of the question, thought Tim.

"In ten seconds the asteroid field will change to a negative charge," warned CAS.

Tim screwed up his eyes and searched in vain for an end to the field, but the orange colour seemed to go on forever.

"Five seconds," announced CAS.

Still there was no end in sight to the field.

"Four seconds . . . three seconds . . . two seconds . . . "

Suddenly they were in the blackness of space again.

"We're out, we're clear!" shouted Tim, and he laughed out loud.

Behind him, the asteroid field flicked to an angry red colour.

Tim glanced at the radar hand sweeping around the screen. The crackle of the asteroid field was still there, but the bleeps of the pursuing Rylons had disappeared.

"I detected a strange irregularity in your breathing as we cleared the asteroid field," said CAS.

"That was a laugh, CAS," explained Tim.

"The word 'laugh' is not contained in my memory banks," said CAS. "Please explain."

"Never mind," said Tim. "Set course for Command ship."

"I am attempting to calculate co-ordinates to enable me to set course," replied CAS. "However, we are now outside our solar system and our current position is not contained on the charts in my memory bank."

"In other words, we're lost," said Tim.

Out of Fuel

"Cut engines," ordered Tim.

There was the usual jerk, as the fighter came to a halt.

"Where do we go from here, CAS?" asked Tim.

"I have taken note of our position before we entered the asteroid field, the angle of the field and the angle of our exit from the field," said CAS. "Based on that information, I have now estimated our position and plotted a course back to our solar system."

"Well then, let's go," said Tim.

"Our fuel supply has been depleted," warned CAS. "At full speed, we have only enough fuel in our main tanks for three minutes and twenty-three seconds flying time."

Tim thought for a moment.

"Set course at half speed, automatic pilot," he decided.

"Course and speed set," confirmed CAS.

Tim stared out through the glass window of the cockpit. The red glow of the asteroid field quickly slipped out of sight and then there was nothing but blackness.

Just over seven minutes later, a red warning light flashed in the middle of the instrument panel.

"Fuel in main tanks has now been exhausted," said CAS. "Should I switch to reserve tank?"

"How much flying time will that give us?" asked Tim.

"One minute at full speed," replied CAS.

"Cut engines," decided Tim. "Maintain our present course and fire engines at half speed every two minutes for fifteen seconds each time. Keep one fifteen-second blast in reserve."

"I have locked in your instructions," confirmed CAS.

Two minutes later the engines fired to life for fifteen seconds and then cut off again. Two minutes later again, the same thing happened, and continued to happen every two minutes until they were down to their last fifteen seconds of fuel.

"All fuel except our reserve blast has now been exhausted," said CAS.

Tim stared out through the window again, but there was nothing to be seen. He glanced at the radar, but it offered no encouragement. The hand swept round and round the screen without interruption.

Suddenly, a bleep appeared on the screen and was quickly followed by another bleep.

Tim's heart leapt in anticipation.

Maybe it's a patrol out searching for me, he thought, but CAS soon dashed his hope.

"Two fighters approaching," it said. "My scanner identifies them as Rylons."

That's the last thing I need, thought Tim.

"How much power have we remaining in our laser bank?" he asked CAS.

"Enough for a twenty-second continuous blast," CAS informed him. "Should I restart the engines?"

"No," replied Tim, "not yet. I need time to think."

A twenty-second blast of lasers would be enough to destroy the two Rylons, if he could get them into position. Unfortunately fifteen seconds of fuel at half power was not enough to manoeuvre them into such a position. He would have to think of something else.

He glanced at the radar screen. The two Rylons had now separated. One was holding its position, while the other was taking a wide circular course in order to get to the other side of him.

CAS confirmed the positions.

"The Rylons are now attacking from opposite directions," it told Tim. "In eight seconds we will be in their range."

"Hold our present position," instructed Tim. "Tell me when they lock in their lasers."

"Rylon lasers are now locked in," said CAS, a few seconds later. "Three seconds before we are in range."

Tim glanced out of the cockpit. He could see the lights of the Rylon fighters bearing down on him from each side.

"Two seconds," warned CAS. "One second . . . we are now in Rylon laser range."

"Fire engines. Full power. Now!" roared Tim.

He was thrown back against the seat, as the engines gave one final blast and the fighter surged forward.

Streams of laser fire from both Rylons hissed behind the fighter and streaked across open space before they exploded against the first objects they met; the Rylon fighters.

"Yes!" shouted Tim in triumph, as two bright flashes in the blackness of space told him that the Rylons had destroyed each other.

CAS did not share his excitement.

"We are now completely out of fuel," it announced.

Tim slumped back in his seat. There was nothing to do now but wait and hope.

He glanced at the radar screen. Once again the hand swept round and round without interruption. He lifted his eyes from the radar and stared blankly straight ahead out through the cockpit glass. A star, numerous light-years away, twinkled in the centre of the window.

Tim didn't know how long he sat staring like that. It could have been ten minutes but the rumblings of hunger in his stomach told him that it was probably a lot longer. I wish I'd brought something to eat, he thought.

The fighter too, felt strangely different.

Before, they had been suspended motionless in space, but now the fighter appeared to be drifting ever so slowly. Tim glanced at the distant twinkling star. It was no longer in the centre of the window, but far over to the left, and moving further and further to the left every second.

So we are moving, thought Tim.

"What's going on, CAS?" he demanded.

"We are being pulled at an angle of thirty-six degrees," said CAS. "Our rate of movement began at

.01 miles per demihour, but has increased constantly. We are now drifting at .1 miles per demihour."

"What's causing it?" asked Tim.

"It appears to be some kind of gravitational pull," CAS told him. "I have scanned the source of the gravity, but my scanners have failed to show up anything."

The twinkling star had now disappeared from the front window. Tim had to turn his head to the left to see it through the side window.

"Angle of drift is remaining constant at thirty-six degrees," advised CAS. "However, we are continuing to accelerate. We are now travelling at .8 miles per demihour."

"Travelling," repeated Tim, but travelling where? he wondered.

CAS seemed to anticipate his silent question.

"I have now located the source of the gravitational pull," it confirmed, "and using all the information available to me, I can now estimate its conformity."

"Well, what is it?" asked Tim impatiently.

"It appears to be a neutrally-charged vacuumed perforation of the cortex of a planet within this solar system," announced CAS.

"I wish you wouldn't talk like that," said Tim irritably. "Please, just tell me what it is?"

"It has been called a gateway to nowhere and a door to the unknown," replied CAS, "but you humans commonly refer to it as 'a black hole'."

A Black Hole

Tim gulped.

"A black hole!" he exclaimed. "I didn't know that they existed."

"Unfortunately they do exist," confirmed CAS.

"What do we know about them?" asked Tim.

"If by 'we' you mean you and I," replied CAS snootily, "then the answer is that I have very little information contained in my memory banks, but I suspect that you know nothing at all."

"OK then, tell me what you know," demanded Tim.

"As far as it is known, a black hole is a collapsed star," explained CAS. "Where once matter and gravity existed together, now only the gravity remains. It is like having a giant vacuum cleaner in space. Any object unlucky enough to drift into its path is sucked in. It is not known if the black hole digests its victims or passes them out the far side into some other galaxy light years away. Either way, nobody has ever returned to tell the tale."

"But we're going to find out," concluded Tim sadly.

"It seems so," agreed CAS. "It will be an interesting experience. However, it is one that we are unlikely to survive."

How ironic, thought Tim; I am about to have a unique experience, but I won't survive to be able to talk about it.

"We are continuing to accelerate," advised CAS. "We are now travelling at 1.5 miles per demihour."

Tim sat back in his seat and closed his eyes. There was nothing else he could do. He felt strangely at peace, like a man waiting for the end to come. But his peace was interrupted by CAS suddenly springing to life again.

"We have stopped accelerating," it said. "We are now moving at a steady speed of 2 miles per demihour."

"Is that a good sign?" asked Tim hopefully.

"It means that we have slipped over the rim and are now in the confines of the black hole," explained CAS.

So we're in its mouth, thought Tim despairingly. Very soon we're going to slip down its throat and discover whatever dark secrets are hidden in its stomach.

A bleep at the very top of the radar screen suddenly lifted Tim out of his despair and gave him new hope.

He watched anxiously as the hand swept around the radar screen. Bleep. It appeared again.

"What is it, CAS?" he whispered.

"My scanners identify it as the Command ship *Alpha I*," replied CAS.

"We're saved, we're saved!" shouted Tim. "Open communications channel."

"I have already tried to contact *Alpha I*," said CAS, "however, our signal is being reflected back to us. It appears that the perimeter of the black hole is acting as some kind of shield."

Tim looked at the bleep as it made its way across the top of the radar screen.

"Can they see us?" he asked CAS.

"We are not within sight, physically," explained CAS, "but we are well within their radar range."

Still the bleep continued in a straight line across the top of the screen.

"Then why don't they turn?" wondered Tim out loud.

"It is possible that the black hole is also blocking their radar signal," said CAS.

"So they don't know we're here," concluded Tim.

"It appears so," agreed CAS.

The bleep of the Command ship continued to move across the radar screen.

Tim looked hopelessly around the cockpit.

There must be something I can do to draw their attention, he thought.

The bleep was now starting to move further away from them.

"Isn't there anything we can do, CAS?" he pleaded.

"I have tried to communicate on a number of occasions, but each time our signal has been reflected back," said CAS. "I have also scanned *Alpha I*, however they do not appear to be picking up our scan."

Suddenly a dot on the radar, close to the bleep of the Command ship, caught Tim's eye. He stared at the screen as the radar hand swept around again. There was the dot, and then beside it the bleep of the Command ship.

"What's causing that dot?" he asked.

"I have scanned the object to which you refer," said CAS. "It is a small piece of metal type 485B. This is the metal used in almost every spacecraft. It is probably a piece of debris from a crashed craft and will not cause us any concern."

"It may not cause us concern," agreed Tim, "but it could be of some use to us. How much laser power have we left?"

"We still have enough for a twenty-second continuous blast," CAS advised him.

If I can hit the debris with our lasers it might draw the Command ship's attention, thought Tim.

The piece of debris was outside Tim's visual range, so he had to use CAS to position the lasers.

"Calculate its position and lock in lasers," ordered Tim.

"Position marked and lasers locked in," confirmed CAS.

"Fire!"

A blast of laser fire shot from the front of the fighter and disappeared into the blackness of space. Far in the distance a small flash appeared, to signify the destruction of the debris.

"Piece of debris destroyed," confirmed CAS, but Tim wasn't listening. He was staring at the radar screen. The bleep of the Command ship had now stopped moving.

Well, at least they've seen the explosion, he thought, but what are they going to do now?

Slowly the bleep began to move again, but this time it did not move across the screen. Instead it began to move in the direction of the fighter.

"They're coming to get us," shouted Tim excitedly. "They're coming to get us!"

"I must remind you that the Command ship cannot pick us up on their radar," warned CAS, "and we are continuing to slip deeper into the black hole."

"As soon as they come into visual range, turn on every light we have," said Tim.

He glanced at the radar screen. The bleep of the Command ship was continuing in a straight line towards them, although when he stared out the window into space there was no sign of it. The blackness seemed to go on forever.

"Hurry up. Please hurry up," pleaded Tim.

A few seconds later, a dull dot appeared far in the distance. As it got closer the light got brighter and brighter, until Tim could see that it was not just one light, but a cluster of small lights. They were the lights of the Command ship.

"We are now within visual range of the Command ship *Alpha I*," confirmed CAS, and at the same time a bright light at the front of the fighter blazed into life.

A light at the front of the Command ship flashed three times in response.

"They've seen us!" yelled Tim.

Gradually the Command ship came closer and

closer, then suddenly, it stopped. Again the light at the front of the ship flashed, but this time in a series of short and long flashes.

"Why did they stop? What do the signals mean?" demanded Tim.

"*Alpha I* is using a signal code called Romse," explained CAS. "It consists of a series of long and short flashes."

It's just like Morse code, thought Tim.

"They have stopped because they have reached the edge of the black hole and it is unsafe for them to proceed any further," continued CAS. "We have slipped too far into the black hole for them to pull us out on a traction beam, so they will have to try to attach an old-fashioned grappling-iron and cable to us. It is a very crude method, and I advise you to hold on tight as we may experience some turbulence."

Tim gripped the side of the seat tightly and waited.

Suddenly, there was a shot from the Command ship and the grappling-iron came swirling towards them. Every nut and bolt in the fighter rattled and shook as the grappling iron hit. Tim shuddered from head to toe as the vibration of the impact shot through him.

Once again the light at the front of the Command ship flashed.

"Grappling-iron is in place," confirmed CAS. "They will now try to pull us clear."

The Command ship reversed until the cable became taut. Even from within his cockpit, Tim could hear the groan of the cable as it strained under pressure.

"We are starting to slow," announced CAS. "We are now travelling at .001 kilomiles per demihour, .0005, .0001, .00005, we have now stopped."

For a few seconds nothing happened, as the might of the Command ship fought against the invisible power of the black hole. All the time the cable remained taut and strained. Then, very slowly, the fighter began to move forward, as the Command ship started to win the battle.

Tim punched the air and laughed out loud.

"They're pulling us clear," he shouted.

"Is that another laugh I detected in your breathing?" asked CAS.

"It certainly was," said Tim.

The black hole did not give up its prey easily. It made the Command ship work hard to regain control of the fighter, but inch by inch the Command ship pulled Tim's craft clear.

At last came the announcement that Tim had been waiting for.

"We are now clear of the black hole," confirmed CAS.

The grappling-iron was released and the traction beam pulled the fighter safely into the hangar. Some of the Command ship crew pushed Tim's fighter into its bay.

When Tim climbed out of the fighter, Uli was there waiting for him.

"We thought you were lost forever," he said.

"So did I," said Tim.

"The Commander wants to see you, but first of all you can have a rest," said Uli.

"And something to eat," added Tim. Trying to escape from the black hole had made him forget about his hunger, but now the rumblings in his stomach had returned to remind him.

Space Station II

Some time later, after a good rest and a good meal, Tim was taken to the bridge to see Commander Ford.

As usual, the Commander and his two generals were sitting at the glass-topped table. They were delighted to see that Tim had returned safe and sound.

"You had quite an adventure," said the Commander.

"I certainly did," agreed Tim, and he went on to tell the Commander everything that had happened.

"Well done, Captain Tim, I knew you were the person we needed," said the commander when Tim was finished telling his story. Then he sat back in his chair and folded his arms as Tim had noticed he always did when he was worried.

"I'm afraid there's another problem," he said gravely.

He pressed a button at the side of the table and the glass top lit up. This time a large round satellite appeared, with six long flat stabilisers jutting out from it.

"This is our fuel depot, *Space Station II*, where we

must refuel before we proceed to *Earth III*," Commander Ford explained. "As you can see, everything seems to be in order. All is quiet, but that unfortunately is the problem – it is *too* quiet.

"The scanners are not showing up any movement on board the station. We have tried to call the crew on a number of occasions, but they have failed to respond. There may be a simple reason for it but, to tell you the truth, I'm worried. Will you check the station out before we dock?"

"Of course I will," agreed Tim.

"That's good," said the Commander. "CAS will give you any information you need to help you get on board."

It didn't take Tim long to get back to the fighter hangar and climb into the freshly refuelled fighter again. When he was safely seated, Uli pulled the cockpit closed.

"Be careful," he warned.

"Don't worry, I will," promised Tim as he clicked his seat belt shut.

Once more, the fighter moved smoothly out of its docking bay, across the hangar floor and out into open space.

"Set co-ordinates for *Space Station II*," said Tim.

"Course set," confirmed CAS.

Although Tim was prepared for the sudden burst of acceleration, he was still thrown back in his seat.

"How long will the journey take?" he asked, when he was sitting upright again.

"One minute and eighteen seconds," calculated CAS.

Just over a minute later, a bleep appeared on the radar screen.

"We are now approaching *Space Station II*," announced CAS. "I have tried to communicate with the crew, but there has been no reply and my scanners are showing no sign of life."

Tim could now see the spacestation approaching quickly. It was much larger than he had expected, like a mini globe hanging in space, with its long flat stabilisers stretching out for hundreds of yards.

"How do I get on board?" asked Tim.

"I am on course for the bottom of the sphere, where the entrance to the docking and refuelling bay is situated," replied CAS.

The fighter slowed and dipped below one of the stabilisers. In front of them appeared the docking and refuelling bay, with its huge doors invitingly open.

Tim could see that the lights were on in the bay. It looked very welcoming, almost too welcoming. Something deep down in his guts made him feel suspicious.

"Stop!" he yelled, and immediately the fighter came to a halt. Tim could not think of any rational reason for his decision, except that sometimes it is better to follow your instincts.

"Is there any other way of getting on board?" he asked.

"There is an emergency hatch on the far side of the space station," CAS informed him.

"Take me to it," ordered Tim.

The fighter turned slowly, slipped under another stabiliser and circled the space station until they came to a circular hatch about the size of a manhole cover. In the centre of the hatch there was a small wheel.

A flap at the front of the fighter, and another at the back flipped open. Two suction cups slid out, attached themselves to the side of the space station, and pulled the fighter in closer.

"We are now secured to *Space Station II*," confirmed CAS. "However, I must warn you that this cockpit is pressurised. When you step outside the cockpit you will be in an unpressurised area. We have no oxygen tanks on board, so you will be unable to breathe and you will float away unless you hold on to something secure.

"The wheel on the emergency hatch turns anticlockwise. You will then be in the decompression chamber. The door from this chamber will not open until the pressure in it equals the pressure in the space station.

"I suggest you take a deep breath, as you will unable to breathe for approximately thirty seconds."

"Thanks, CAS," said Tim.

He gulped down as much air as his lungs would hold before sliding back the roof of the cockpit. With his hands on the seat, he pushed his head and shoulders out into space. He suddenly felt a strange cold, numbing sensation on the exposed skin of his face. It was like being under water in a very cold pool, but without the water.

With both hands he gripped the wheel of the emergency hatch and pulled himself out of the cockpit. Immediately his legs began to drift up, up, up. Soon they were far above his head.

Luckily I'm holding on tight, thought Tim.

He tried to turn the wheel, but it wouldn't move. He tried it again; it still wouldn't move. With a great heave and gasp, he put in one tremendous effort. The wheel turned, but at the same time his lungs emptied. Automatically he opened his mouth to fill his lungs again, but there was no air. A pain started deep down in his chest and started to move up towards his throat. He felt himself starting to choke and his head felt light and dizzy. He wanted to close his eyes, let go the wheel and drift away into space. Only CAS's continuous warning stopped him.

"Keep turning the wheel. Keep turning the wheel," it repeated over and over again, through the intercom on Tim's suit.

Somehow Tim found the strength to obey CAS's instruction. He turned the wheel again and pushed with all his failing strength. Reluctantly the hatch swung open. Tim crawled into the decompression chamber, slammed the hatch behind him and slumped against the entrance door to the space station.

"Come in, Captain Tim. Captain Tim, come in," CAS's voice bubbled from Tim's intercom and echoed round and round the chamber.

Tim's mouth opened and closed, like a fish out of water, as he gasped for breath. The pain got more and more severe. It felt like his chest was going to burst.

"Come in, Captain Tim," called CAS again, but Tim could only gasp in reply.

Suddenly, the chamber door sprang open, and Tim fell sprawling on to the space station floor. The sweet taste of air rushed down his throat and filled his lungs. His chest heaved and fell and gradually the pain and the pressure eased.

"Come in, Captain Tim. Come in, Captain Tim," CAS continued to call over the intercom.

"It's OK, CAS," panted Tim. "I've made it."

Tim scrambled to his feet when his breathing returned to near normal.

"I seem to be in the control room," he told CAS, as he glanced around the room, "but there's nobody here."

"In the corner of the room there is a spiral staircase," said CAS. "It will take you down to the docking and refuelling bay."

"I can see it," confirmed Tim.

Tim passed the control desk on his way across the room. As he started down the spiral stairs, something black under the desk caught his eye. It was a shoe. Tim bent down and picked it up. The front of the shoe was badly burnt and there was a strong bitter smell like the smell of burnt hair. Tim pressed the button on his collar and described the shoe and smell to CAS.

"That is one of the crew's shoes," said CAS. "It sounds like he was vaporised by a Rylon laser gun."

Tim dropped the shoe where he had found it and went down the spiral staircase until he came to the large docking and refuelling bay. He pressed the button on his collar again.

"I am now in the docking bay," he told CAS. "There is no sign of any of the crew or any Rylons."

"Can you see the pump house?" asked CAS.

Tim's eyes flashed around the bay until they came to rest on a green door with the words "Pump House" written on it.

"I can see it," he told CAS.

"On the wall beside the door there are gauges," said CAS. "They will tell you how much fuel is in the tanks."

Tim strolled across the bay and glanced at the gauges. There were four in all. He pressed the button on his collar.

"They are all reading full," he told CAS.

"Should I tell the Command ship to come in and dock?" asked CAS.

"Not yet," said Tim. "I want to have another quick look around."

Tim checked everywhere on the space station but, apart from the burnt shoe, there was no sign of the crew or the Rylons.

He contacted CAS again.

"Tell the Command ship that it's all clear," he said.

Tim stood in the bay and watched the Command ship approach. Everything was going smoothly. In less than one minute, the Command ship would dock, but Tim still felt worried.

Why had the Rylons come on board and vaporised the crew, but left the fuel intact? It just didn't make sense. Why hadn't they simply blown up the spacestation?

The questions swam round and round in Tim's head.

Suddenly, something on the right side of the docking bay caught his attention. It was a small black box. He glanced over to the left side. There was another black box, and between them was a thin beam of blue light. It could only be one thing, a laser booby-trap.

Booby-trap

"Stop!" Tim roared into the intercom. "Tell the Command ship to stop."

Tim stood helplessly in the docking bay and watched in agony as the Command ship inched its way closer to the deadly blue line. If it broke the laser beam, they would all be blown to smithereens.

"Why aren't they stopping, CAS?" he demanded.

"The Command ship has reversed its engines," CAS told him. "The crew are stopping it as quickly as they can."

Still the Command ship came closer and closer, until finally it shuddered to a halt less than a foot from the laser beam.

Tim sighed with relief.

"I am putting you directly through to Commander Ford," announced CAS.

There was a pause for a few seconds, before the Commander's calm voice came through.

"What's wrong, Tim?" he asked.

"There's a laser beam across the entrance to the bay," said Tim, and he went on to describe the two black boxes.

"It is a laser booby-trap, right enough," agreed the Commander. "One of the black boxes must contain the switch. You will have to open the boxes carefully until you find the switch and then try to disconnect it."

Tim decided to start with the box on the right side of the bay, because that was the nearest one to him.

The lid of the box was held in place by two screws. Tim pulled the utility knife from his pocket and flipped out the screwdriver.

Slowly and carefully he turned the screws until they were loose, then he gently prised off the lid.

There was a printed circuit inside the box which reminded him of the inside of the remote control for the video. He pressed the intercom button on his suit and described the printed circuit to Commander Ford.

"The switch must be in the other box," decided the Commander.

Tim walked across the bay to the other box, making sure he kept well clear of the laser beam. This box was exactly the same as the box on the right side, with two screws holding the lid in place.

Once again he carefully loosened the screws and lifted off the lid.

This time, instead of a printed circuit, there were two small metal plates, each about one inch long and a half inch wide. One plate was slightly above the other, and there were two white wires connected to the top plate.

In the corner of the box there was something even more sinister. It was a small digital watch and, even as Tim looked at it, the numbers decreased every second. Thirty-five . . . thirty-four . . . thirty-three . . .

Tim pressed the button on the collar of his suit again.

"I've found the switch," he told the Commander, "but there is a timer on it. I must have triggered it when I came on board."

"What does the switch look like?" asked Commander Ford.

Tim described the metal plates and the wires.

"One of the wires will detonate the device and the other one will disarm it," advised the Commander.

"How will I know which one is which?" asked Tim.

"You will have to make that decision yourself," said the Commander, "but whichever wire you choose, you must cut it before you run out of time."

Tim glanced at the watch. The seconds descended steadily, twenty . . . nineteen . . . eighteen . . .

He flipped the screwdriver back into place, and unfolded the scissors part of the utility knife.

There must be some way of knowing which wire to cut, he thought. But both wires looked exactly the same. One wire was connected to the top of the plate – that one would be easy to cut. The other wire was connected to the bottom of the plate – that one would be more awkward to cut.

The time on the watch continued to tick away. Fourteen . . . thirteen . . . twelve . . .

Tim tried to concentrate.

Which way would I connect the wires if I was setting up a trap? he thought. Would I make the disarming wire easy or awkward to cut? I think I'd make it awkward to cut, he decided.

He slipped the blades of the scissors around the bottom wire and glanced at the watch. He was almost out of time. Five . . . four . . . three . . . it was now or never.

His stomach fluttered and a trickle of nervous sweat ran down his forehead and stopped at the tip of his nose. He squeezed the scissors and prayed silently. The wire snapped. The watch stopped, and the blue laser beam disappeared.

"I did it!" shouted Tim in delight and relief. "I did it!"

Preparing for Battle

After refuelling, the Command ship set a course for *Earth III*. Meanwhile, Tim tried to get some sleep in the pilots' quarters.

As they approached *Earth III*, Uli woke Tim and took him to the bridge for a briefing. As usual, the Commander and his generals were sitting at the glass-topped table.

"We have almost reached our destination, Captain Tim," said Commander Ford, and he pressed a button at the side of the table.

This time, instead of the glass top lighting up, two panels on the wall of the bridge slid open to reveal a large screen. The screen flickered twice before it finally lit up.

In the corner of the screen, Tim could see a globe, which looked like a mini Earth, but in front of the globe there was a sinister looking black starship.

"This is *Earth III*," explained the Commander, "where five million people are depending on us. By our calculations, they are now completely out of fresh water. This is the Rylon *Destroyer*," the Commander pointed to the black starship. "As you can see, there is no way we can land on *Earth III* without first getting by the *Destroyer*, and in order to do that we must defeat the Rylons."

Commander Ford sat back and folded his arms.

"I will be honest with you, Captain Tim," he said seriously. "So far, we have had no success in our battles with the Rylon *Destroyer*. In fact we have never even got close enough to hit it with our lasers. Its guns are so powerful and so accurate, that they blast our fighters out of space before they can even get in range."

"Maybe it'll be different this time," said Tim.

"I hope so," said the Commander, "but we have only thirteen fighters, including yours, operational. It is a huge task to ask them to take on."

"We will give it our best shot, Commander," Tim assured him.

"I know you will," agreed the Commander. "In less than ten minutes we will be close enough to the Rylon *Destroyer* to launch an attack. In the meantime, I think you should meet the other pilots and formulate some kind of plan of attack."

Uli and Tim left the bridge and went back down to the pilots' quarters. The pilots were sitting on a circular seat waiting for them. Twelve pairs of eyes stared at Tim when he entered the room. All the other pilots were older than himself, and Tim felt worried about giving them orders.

What happens if they don't want to fly with me? he thought, but he need not have worried. Suddenly, one by one all the pilots stood up, applauded and cheered.

"They have heard about your battles with the Rylons," explained Uli. "They are all proud to fly with you."

Tim smiled with relief.

Well, at least that's that out of the way, he thought.

The applause and the cheers died away and the pilots waited for Tim to speak.

"In a few minutes we will be facing the greatest task of our lives," he began. "As you know, *Earth III* is under siege, and the people have now run out of water. We must get the purification crystals through to them, and to do that we must first knock out the Rylon *Destroyer*."

Tim paused for a few moments. His throat felt dry. He swallowed to relieve the dryness.

"The people of *Earth III* are depending on us," he continued, "but the task of knocking out the Rylon *Destroyer* is a dangerous one, and many of us may not return."

Tim looked at each pilot in turn.

"I will understand if some of you do not want to fly on this mission," he said.

"We'll fly with you, Captain Tim," shouted the twelve pilots with one voice.

"Good," said Tim. "Now we must get organised, we haven't much time left. I will divide you into two squadrons of six, a Green Squadron and a Red Squadron. I will lead the attack. You should keep in intercom contact at all times and watch closely everything that I do."

The Battle Rages

Tim and the other pilots stood beside their fighters, waiting for the word to attack. Tim could feel the Command ship gradually getting slower and slower, until it finally stopped.

A loudspeaker on the wall above the fighters crackled into life, and Commander Ford's voice filled the hangar.

"The Command ship can go no further in safety," the Commander told them. "From here on you are on your own. Take care, and good luck."

"OK, men, let's go," said Tim. "It's up to us now."

The pilots climbed into their fighters and the glass cockpit tops were pulled across and closed.

One by one, the fighters glided smoothly out of their bays, slid across the hangar floor, and out through the door into open space.

Tim moved to the front of the column.

"Red Squadron to my left, Green Squadron to my right," he ordered. "Set course for *Earth III* and move out at half speed."

The fighters blasted off smoothly, in the shape of an arrow-head, with Tim at the front.

"Keep in close formation," he warned.

In the distance, he could see *Earth III*. Across its surface lay a large foreboding shadow, cast by the eerie dark object hovering in front of it – the Rylon *Destroyer*.

Tim glanced at the radar screen. There was a large crackling bleep, as the sweeping hand picked up *Earth III* and the Rylon *Destroyer*. Suddenly the radar screen became dotted with a number of other, smaller, bleeps. Tim counted eighteen in all.

"Three squadrons of Rylon fighters coming to intercept us," warned CAS.

"Hold your positions," Tim instructed the other pilots through his intercom.

The eighteen bleeps on the radar screen divided into three squadrons of six. One squadron went to the right, one squadron went to the left and one squadron stayed in the centre.

So they're up to their old tricks again, thought Tim.

"Ten seconds until we come into Rylon laser range," warned CAS.

"Continue to hold your positions," Tim instructed the pilots again. He could now see the lights of the Rylon fighters approaching quickly.

"Seven seconds," said CAS, "six seconds . . . five . . . "

"Single line formation," ordered Tim. "Red Squadron first."

The Red Squadron moved to the right, and the Green Squadron to the left, until they were all in one long column.

"Three seconds to Rylon range," warned CAS. "Two seconds . . . one second . . . Rylon lasers locked."

"Full power and dive at forty-five degrees," roared Tim.

He pushed the control handles and the fighter surged and dived. Behind him the rest of the pilots did the same, and the whole column dived in one movement as if it was an extension of Tim's fighter.

Stream after stream of Rylon laser fire streaked harmlessly above the column of Federation fighters. The Rylon strategy was in disarray and, before they had time to adjust their formation, Tim had issued another order.

"Climb, forty-five degrees," he shouted and pulled hard on the controls. Immediately his fighter began to climb, and behind him the other fighters also climbed.

"The Rylons are now within our laser range," CAS informed him.

"Break formation and attack," ordered Tim. "Let's show them how Federation pilots can fight."

A Rylon fighter drifted across Tim's flight path. He adjusted the right control handle until he had the Rylon in the middle of his sights, then he pressed the firing button. A burst of laser fire shot from the front of his fighter and hit the Rylon dead centre. There was a flash, and the Rylon disintegrated before his eyes.

What had been quiet open space between the Command ship and the Rylon *Destroyer* was now the stage of a raging battle. Federation and Rylon fighters streaked across space as the battle reached its height. Laser fire crisscrossed in intricate patterns as fighter fought fighter. Smoke billowed and swirled from damaged fighters, and the blackness of space was continuously lit up by blinding flashes, as fighters were blown to pieces.

Tim's radar screen was a mass of bleeps, and he had to rely on sight to distinguish Rylon fighters from Federation fighters.

"Rylon fighter on our tail," warned CAS.

Tim pulled hard on the controls and the fighter climbed steeply.

"Rylon fighter is still pursuing us," advised CAS, "and his lasers are now locked in."

"Reverse engines," ordered Tim.

There was a screech, as the engine suddenly changed direction and the fighter shot backwards.

The Rylon was taken by surprise, and before he could react he had flashed past Tim's fighter.

"Engines forward," shouted Tim.

There was another screech as the engines changed direction again, and the fighter surged forward in pursuit of the Rylon.

Tim manoeuvred the right control handle until the centre of the fleeing Rylon appeared in the middle of his sights. He pressed the firing button and a stream of laser fire streaked through space. But at the last moment the Rylon swerved and, instead of hitting the centre of the target, the volley caught the rear of the fighter. The back panel was blown off and the fighter was sent spinning out of control.

"I won't miss this time," said Tim and he twisted the control handle until once more the Rylon appeared in his sights. This time he pressed the button twice. Two bursts of laser fire found their target and the Rylon disappeared in a blazing inferno.

"Help!" The plea screamed through Tim's intercom. "This is Red fighter III. I am being pursued by two Rylons and I can't shake them off. Please help!"

"Where are you, Red fighter III?" asked Tim.

"I am at sixty-seven degrees north by twenty-two degrees west," came the reply.

Tim glanced at the sweeping hand of the radar screen. Three bleeps appeared at the co-ordinates he had just been given.

"I can see you, Red fighter III," confirmed Tim. "I'm on my way."

Tim pushed the left control and set the fighter on course to meet Red fighter III. In a few seconds he was in visual range.

Red fighter III was doing everything he could to shake off the Rylons, but by now they were almost on top of him. Their laser fire flashed on every side of the Federation craft. Tim knew that the pilot would not be able to hold on much longer.

"Turn sixty degrees west," instructed Tim.

The pilot of Red fighter III followed Tim's instructions immediately. As he turned at a sixty-degree angle, the chasing Rylons were dragged into Tim's path.

Tim adjusted the sights until he had locked in on the first of the Rylons. He pressed the firing button. A burst of laser fire hit its target and the Rylon disappeared in a bright flash.

The other Rylon now tried to run for it, but Tim and Red fighter III were soon on his tail.

"Have you got him in your sights?" asked Tim.

"I have," confirmed the pilot of Red fighter III.

"Fire!" shouted Tim and at the same time he pressed his firing button.

The Rylon was caught by the laser fire of both fighters and blown to pieces.

A strange pattern on the radar screen caught Tim's eye. At the top of the screen, a group of seven bleeps had gathered in a little cluster and had started to move in the direction of the Rylon *Destroyer*.

"The surviving Rylon fighters are retreating," confirmed CAS.

"How many fighters did we lose?" asked Tim.

"Three of our fighters have been destroyed," CAS told him. "We have ten fighters operational, including this one."

"Red Squadron and Green Squadron regroup and follow me," instructed Tim through the intercom. "Do not shoot the retreating Rylons. I repeat, do not shoot the retreating Rylons."

If we stay behind the Rylon fighters, they will act as a shield and lead us in close to the *Destroyer*, thought Tim.

"We are now within Rylon *Destroyer* laser cannon range," warned CAS. "I urge caution."

"Fly in close formation," Tim instructed the other pilots. "Keep the Rylon fighters between you and the *Destroyer* at all times, and hold your fire."

The pilots immediately obeyed Tim's instructions, and the Federation fighters huddled together in a small group behind the Rylons.

"Rylon *Destroyer* lasers are now locked in," warned CAS.

But they can't shoot while their fighters are in the way, thought Tim.

Suddenly, the blackness of space was shattered by a barrage of flashes and laser beams which cut through the darkness. It was like a fireworks display on Hallowe'en, except this was real.

Three Rylon fighters were blown to smithereens in the initial barrage.

Tim couldn't believe his eyes.

They have opened fire on their own fighters, he thought in disbelief. The Rylon *Destroyer* has actually shot down its own fighters.

"Hold your positions," instructed Tim. "We're almost in range."

There was another barrage of laser fire from the Rylon *Destroyer*. This time, two more Rylon fighters went down.

"Break formation and attack," Tim roared into the intercom.

The Federation fighters stretched out in a straight line and launched their attack on the Rylon *Destroyer*. The two remaining Rylon fighters tried to turn to face the attackers, but they were soon blown out of existence.

Tim stared at the great dark mass of the Rylon *Destroyer* looming in front of him. Even the sight of it sent a shiver of fear down his spine.

"Lock lasers," he instructed CAS.

"Lasers locked," confirmed CAS.

"Fire."

Volley after volley of laser fire from Tim's cannons crashed against the *Destroyer*, but all to no avail. Tim could hardly believe what he was seeing. The laser fire just bounced off the hard shell of the *Destroyer* and was deflected harmlessly into open space.

The *Destroyer* now lit up in a pattern of flames and flashes as every gun on it sprang to life and illuminated space like a town on Christmas Eve.

The Federation fighters tried to dodge the exploding lasers as they continued their attack. Tim's fighter rocked and shuddered from the impact of lasers exploding nearby.

"Green fighter III and Red fighter V have been destroyed," CAS informed Tim.

Tim tried to concentrate on the huge target in front of him.

"Fire lasers," he commanded.

Once more the lasers registered a direct hit, but once more they bounced harmlessly off the *Destroyer.*

"Green fighter IV has been hit," advised CAS.

Tim could see that it was no use continuing their attack. Their lasers were having no effect on the *Destroyer.*

"Break off attack," he ordered. "All fighters return to Command ship."

As Tim turned to retreat, he notice a thin whiff of smoke coming from underneath the Rylon *Destroyer.*

"Did we damage the *Destroyer*?" he asked CAS hopefully.

"The smoke you see is from the *Destroyer*'s burnt fuel fumes outlet," CAS informed him. "It is not a result of our laser fire."

"You mean it's their exhaust pipe," said Tim.

As they flew back towards the Command ship, Tim

kept thinking about the exhaust pipe, until an idea suddenly clicked in his brain. A burnt fuel fumes outlet, that's how CAS had described it, he thought. And there was only one place those fumes could come from – the engine.

The more he thought about it, the more the idea began to evolve into a plan.

Tim's Plan

The seven remaining Federation fighters got back to the Command ship safely and parked in their bays.

Tim pulled back the cockpit roof and climbed out of the fighter. His feet had barely touched the ground when Uli came running up to him.

"The Commander wants to see you on the bridge right away," he said.

Commander Ford, General Yore and General Lee were waiting anxiously on the bridge for a report of the attack on the Rylon *Destroyer*.

"I'm afraid we had no luck, Commander," explained Tim. "We lost three fighters trying to get into range, and then our laser fire just bounced off the *Destroyer*."

Commander Ford sighed with disappointment.

"So how are we going to knock it out?" he asked in desperation.

Before Tim had a chance to answer, one of the men sitting at a computer screen on the higher level suddenly swung around.

"Our Radar shows two squadrons of Rylon fighters approaching," said the man.

"Put them on the screen," ordered the Commander.

Once more the two panels slid open and the large screen on the wall of the bridge lit up. The two squadrons of Rylon fighters, who were flying in close formation, could be seen clearly. Suddenly, the twelve Rylons spread out into a straight line and prepared to attack.

"Are our fighters ready for combat again?" asked the Commander.

"They are still being refuelled and repaired," replied the operator.

"We'll have to use the ship's guns for our defence," decided the Commander quickly. "Lock in our laser cannons."

"Cannons are locked in," confirmed a second man at another screen.

"Fire cannons," ordered the Commander.

The Command ship rolled slightly, as the big cannons fired a broadside of laser fire at the oncoming Rylons.

Five flashes appeared on the screen as five Rylon fighters took the brunt of the broadside.

The computer operator confirmed the hits.

"Five Rylon fighters destroyed," he said, "but the remaining Rylons are continuing to attack."

"Lock in laser cannons again," ordered the Commander.

"Laser cannons locked in," confirmed the operator.

"Fire."

Once more the Command ship rolled slightly from the recoil of the broadside.

Four more flashes appeared on the screen, as four more Rylon fighters were annihilated.

"The remaining three Rylon fighters are continuing to attack," warned the operator. "Although we are now within their range, they have not yet fired at us."

"It must be a suicide mission," shouted the Commander. "They have to be stopped! Man every gun. Fire at will."

Every gun on the Command ship blazed to life in an attempt to stop the oncoming Rylons. Another flash appeared on the screen, followed quickly by another, as two more of the Rylon fighters were caught in the frenzied laser fire.

"The remaining Rylon is inside our fire cover," cried the operator. "It's going to hit us."

"Hold on, everybody," advised the Commander.

Tim held on to the back of a chair tightly and waited for the crash. It came a few seconds later. The Command ship shuddered from the impact and men and instruments were flung across the Bridge. Tim's chair spun from his grip. His feet slipped, and the floor seemed to rush up and hit him in the face. The lights went out and the ship was plunged into complete blackness. Men groaned and screamed and shouted and, above all the noise, the Commander shouted loudest.

"Keep calm," he ordered.

The lights fluttered and flickered, and then came back on. The men scrambled back to their positions and Tim staggered to his feet.

"I want a damage report," ordered the Commander.

A third man at a screen gave the information.

"The Rylon has crashed into our engine-room," he told the Commander. "Three of the crew have been slightly injured and our power supply has been damaged."

"What is the extent of the damage?" asked Commander Ford.

"We are reduced to seventy per cent power," said the man, "and we are losing a further five per cent every demihour."

The Commander thought for a few moments.

"We will have to return to *Earth I* and carry out repairs," he decided. General Yore and General Lee nodded in agreement.

"But what about the people on *Earth III*?" asked Tim in amazement. "We can't just leave them."

"I'm afraid we'll have to leave them," said the Commander sadly. "There's nothing more we can do for them. You saw yourself how your laser fire bounced off the *Destroyer*, and now this ship is damaged. We can do no more."

"If I could knock out the *Destroyer*, would you change your mind?" asked Tim.

"Of course I would," replied the Commander, "but how do you propose to do that?"

"I have a plan," explained Tim. "As I was retreating from our attack, I noticed a thin whiff of smoke coming from underneath the *Destroyer*. CAS told me it was an exhaust outlet for the fumes from burnt fuel. I was thinking that, if it is an outlet, then it must also be an inlet."

Tim paused for a moment. The Commander and the two generals were listening intently.

"If I can get a shot down the outlet, I believe it will carry all the way to the engine and disable the *Destroyer*," concluded Tim.

The Commander looked doubtful.

"How will you get close enough to the *Destroyer* to hit your target?" he asked. "They will blow you to pieces before you can get within range."

"I will take two fighters with me," explained Tim. "Being such a small force, the Rylons probably won't launch their fighters. When the *Destroyer* opens fire, I will cut my engines and pretend that I have been hit, but I will continue to float towards the *Destroyer*. The two other fighters will keep up the attack and act as a decoy. Hopefully, the *Destroyer* will concentrate on them and forget about me.

"When I am in close enough, I will fire my engines again and get into a position to get a shot down the outlet. By that time it will be too late for the Rylons to stop me."

"It sounds very dangerous," said the Commander.

"It is," agreed Tim, "but I think it will work."

"What do you think?" Commander Ford asked his two generals.

"It does sound very risky," said General Lee, "but it is our only chance and it just might work."

"I agree," said General Yore. "I think it's worth the risk."

Commander Ford rubbed his chin with the palm of his hand.

"OK, you can go," he agreed reluctantly, "but only if you can get two volunteers to go with you."

"Thank you, sir," said Tim. "We won't let you down."

The Rylon *Destroyer*

Tim returned to the pilots' quarters and outlined his plan to the six other pilots.

"I need two volunteers to fly with me," he explained.

The six pilots answered as one.

"I'll go with you," they all shouted.

After they had tossed many coins, Red fighter I and Red fighter III were selected to go with Tim.

When the two pilots were ready and seated in their fighters, Tim led them across the hangar floor and out into open space.

"Stay close to me," he instructed through his intercom as they blasted off.

Soon they had left the safety of the Command ship far behind them.

Tim kept his eyes on the radar screen, while CAS monitored the situation.

"In thirty seconds we will be within the *Destroyer*'s range," it informed Tim.

Tim watched the radar hand sweep around the screen. Once again there was a large crackling bleep, as the radar picked up *Earth III* and the Rylon

Destroyer, but just as he had hoped, there were no smaller bleeps of Rylon fighters.

So far, so good, he thought.

"Twenty seconds until we are within *Destroyer*'s range," advised CAS.

"Continue to hold your positions," Tim instructed the other pilots.

He glanced at the radar screen again. There was still no sign of Rylon fighters.

"Ten seconds until we are within *Destroyer*'s range," warned CAS.

"I am now going to set a course that will keep us on the outer range limit of the *Destroyer*'s guns," Tim explained to the other pilots. "When the *Destroyer* opens fire, I will cut my engines and float towards it. You should continue on this course to draw the *Destroyer*'s attention."

"Instruction understood," confirmed both pilots.

Tim told CAS the course he wanted to take.

"Course calculated and set," confirmed CAS.

Tim felt the fighter suddenly swerve to the right as it took the new course. Red fighter I and Red fighter III immediately followed.

"I should warn you that the *Destroyer*'s lasers are now locked in," continued CAS, "and in three seconds we will be within their range."

The three seconds seemed to pass in an instant.

"We are now within the *Destroyer*'s range," announced CAS. It had only just given the warning, when space was suddenly illuminated by a bombardment of laser fire from the *Destroyer*.

Tim felt his fighter shudder from the impact of a laser exploding close by.

"Cut engines," he told CAS.

There was a jerk, as the engines died and the fighter began to drift towards the *Destroyer*.

"You're on your own now," Tim advised Red fighter I and Red fighter III.

Laser fire continued to hiss and flash around Tim's fighter.

Nothing I can do now but wait and hope, he thought to himself.

Suddenly the fighter shook and spun violently, and even the seat belt didn't stop Tim from being flung across the cockpit.

"What's happening?" he cried.

"The rear of our fighter was caught in the shock wave of an explosion," explained CAS. "There is no damage to the fighter, but we have been knocked three degrees off course."

"Can we correct that?" asked Tim, when he had scrambled back to his seat.

"Only if we blast our engines," said CAS.

I can't do that, thought Tim. I'll just have to hope that we don't drift too far away from the *Destroyer*.

He glanced at the radar screen. Red fighter I and Red fighter III had now moved away from him and, just as he had planned, they were drawing the Rylon fire. He was safe from the *Destroyer* for as long as they could keep up the attack.

Unfortunately, that wasn't for very long. The two fighters came under heavy fire from the *Destroyer*'s big guns and were forced to retreat.

"Red fighter I and Red fighter III have broken off attack," confirmed CAS. "The Rylon *Destroyer* is now trying to scan us. I am going to shut down all functions and I suggest that you keep as quiet and as still as possible until I give you the all-clear."

Suddenly all the lights on the instrument panel went out and the cockpit was plunged into complete blackness. Only the radar screen remained operational, and on it Tim could see the two fighters moving further and further away.

Tim sat still and waited for what seemed an eternity. The waiting seemed to go forever, until finally CAS came to life again and broke the silence.

"The Rylon *Destroyer* has now completed its scan," it advised Tim.

"They must be satisfied that we are disabled," said Tim, "or else they would have blown us apart. How long before we are in range of the *Destroyer*?"

"At our current speed and course, it will take two minutes and twenty-three seconds," calculated CAS.

That's a long time to wait, thought Tim.

The two bleeps on the radar screen had now turned and were approaching the *Destroyer* again.

"Red fighter I and Red fighter III have resumed their attack," confirmed CAS.

Once more, the two fighters took the course that would keep them on the outer limit of the *Destroyer*'s range. But again the Rylon *Destroyer* bombarded them with laser fire from its big guns.

"One minute and forty seconds before the *Destroyer* comes into our range," advised CAS.

If only they can keep up the attack long enough for

me to get a little closer, thought Tim, but once again the heavy bombardment from the *Destroyer* was too much for the fighters.

"Red fighter I has been hit by laser fire," observed CAS. "One of its jets has been damaged and it is unable to continue with the attack."

A worried voice crackled through Tim's intercom.

"This is the pilot of Red fighter III," said the voice. "The bombardment is getting too heavy. Red fighter I has already been damaged. We will have to retreat. I'm sorry, Captain, but we can do no more."

"You did well," Tim replied over the intercom. "How long will it take before the *Destroyer* comes into our range?" he asked CAS.

"If we continue to drift, it will take one minute and ten seconds," said CAS. "If we fire our engines and attack at full speed it will take eighteen seconds."

The thought of floating helplessly in space for more than another minute, and hoping that the Rylons wouldn't fire on him, didn't appeal to Tim.

"Fire engines and set course for *Destroyer*," he decided. "We'll have to attack and take our chances."

The engines fired to life, and the fighter immediately surged forward in the direction of the *Destroyer*.

Tim gripped the controls firmly and glanced at the Radar screen. Red fighter I and Red fighter III were continuing to move further and further away, while the *Destroyer* was getting closer and closer.

I really am on my own now, he thought.

"Rylon *Destroyer* is attempting to lock in its lasers," warned CAS. "Twelve more seconds before it comes into our range."

Tim could see the lights of the *Destroyer* in the distance.

Any second now they're going to open fire, he thought, and all I can do is keep flying and hoping.

"Rylon lasers locked in," said CAS.

"Switch to manual control," decided Tim.

"Automatic pilot has now been disengaged," confirmed CAS.

Tim moved the right and left control handles at random. The fighter began to zigzag erratically, but kept flying in the direction of the *Destroyer*.

Suddenly the *Destroyer* lit up with twinkling and flashing lights, as every gun on it trained its sights on Tim and opened fire.

The space around Tim's fighter became a mass of streaks and flashes and exploding lasers. Tim had no way of knowing where the next laser would hit. He just kept pulling and pushing the controls and hoping that it wouldn't hit him.

"Eight seconds before the *Destroyer* comes into our range," announced CAS.

A laser flashed in front of Tim. The fighter shuddered. Another laser followed closely behind. Tim pushed the left control. The fighter swerved, but directly into the path of more oncoming lasers.

The fighter shook fiercely and started to spin. Tim's whole body vibrated uncontrollably. A searing pain shot through his left shoulder and down his arm. CAS made another announcement, but its voice was drowned out by Tim's scream of pain and terror.

"I've been hit," he yelled. "I've been hit!"

His left hand fell from the controls. His arm felt

numb and swung uselessly by his side like a pendulum in a clock. His fingers tingled and there was a constant searing pain in his shoulder. He felt dizzy. His head reeled and his eyes burned as the fighter spiralled downwards through the blackness.

"I must get the fighter under control," Tim said to himself.

He reached across with his right arm and lifted his injured hand back on to the control again. He wiggled a finger.

"Ouch!" he yelled, as an agonising pain shot up his arm and into his shoulder.

Tim tried to block out the pain, as one by one he forced each finger to close around the control. But each time a finger closed, the same agonising pain ripped at his arm.

To get the fighter under control he needed to move both controls simultaneously. His left hand just *had* to work. With his good hand he pushed the right control, but when he tried to pull the left control the pain became unbearable. It felt like his arm was being ripped from his shoulder.

"I must do it," he told himself, but the pain in his arm was too severe to overcome.

Once again CAS came to life and gave Tim the encouragement he needed to try again.

"We are now inside the maximum depression range of the *Destroyer*'s guns," it said.

"What does that mean, CAS?" asked Tim.

"Our spiral descent has taken us directly beneath the Rylon *Destroyer*," explained CAS. "For the moment they can't hit us with their laser guns.

However, we will soon drift back into their range again."

It was only then Tim noticed that it was completely black outside. There were no flashing or exploding lasers.

"I must get the fighter under control," he said to himself again.

He gritted his teeth and tried to move the left control. Once more the pain ripped through his arm.

"You can do it, Tim. You can do it," he said over and over to himself.

Sweat ran down his face and his back from the agonising effort, but very slowly the left control began to move. He eased the right control in slightly and gradually the fighter came out of its spin until it was finally back under control again.

"I did it," shouted Tim. "Set course for *Destroyer*'s exhaust outlet," he told CAS.

"Course set," confirmed CAS.

A few seconds later, the huge dark belly of the *Destroyer* loomed up in front of Tim. The *Destroyer* continued its laser bombardment and space was illuminated by their deadly beams, but just as CAS had predicted, they all fell wide of Tim's fighter. He was now in a dark narrow passage that led straight to the Rylon *Destroyer*. And directly in front of him was the exhaust outlet.

Suddenly the *Destroyer* began to move away to Tim's right.

"The *Destroyer* is taking evasive action," warned CAS.

"Keep on course for exhaust outlet," said Tim.

"I have adjusted our flight path in accordance with the movement of the *Destroyer*," said CAS. "However, I must warn you that our present course will take us back into the *Destroyer*'s laser range exactly two seconds after the exhaust outlet comes into our range."

Two seconds, thought Tim. That'll give me just one shot.

"Three seconds until the exhaust outlet comes into our range," advised CAS.

Tim adjusted the right control handle until his target was in the centre of his sights. All around him the Rylon lasers were getting closer and closer to his craft, but Tim continued to concentrate on the exhaust outlet.

"I'm only going to get one chance," he told himself, "and I'll have to make it count."

"Two seconds to range," announced CAS. "One second . . . "

Tim's thumb hovered above the firing button. He kept the exhaust in the centre of his sights and waited for CAS to give the signal. That signal came one second later.

"*Destroyer* exhaust outlet now in range," said CAS.

Tim depressed the firing button firmly. A stream of laser fire streaked across space towards the *Destroyer*.

Some of the lasers ricocheted off the hard shell of the *Destroyer*, but most found their target and disappeared down the exhaust outlet.

"Let's get out of here, CAS," said Tim.

The fighter swerved sharply away from the

Destroyer, but straight into the line of fire of its guns. Lasers flashed menacingly around Tim's craft, then suddenly stopped.

Space went still and black. Tim couldn't hear or see anything, except for the sweeping hand of the radar.

Suddenly, there was a blinding flash behind him which lit up space as if it were the middle of the day, and a ball of flame mushroomed up from the middle of the *Destroyer*, spreading out in all directions.

The incredible force of the blast sent shock waves ripping through space. Tim's fighter vibrated violently from the pressure of the shock waves. A pain shot through his back, as if someone had dropped a heavy weight on him. His injured arm throbbed agonisingly and fell from the control. He felt like his whole body was going to explode.

For almost ten seconds he shook uncontrollably then, gradually, the pressure eased and so too did the pain in his back. Tim slumped back in his seat and stared at the radar screen.

As the hand swept around the screen there was just a single bleep – *Earth III*.

Suddenly, two smaller bleeps appeared at the top of the screen. Tim sat up straight, but then relaxed again when a familiar voice crackled through his intercom.

"This is Red fighter III," said the voice. "Are you all right, Captain Tim?"

"Just a bit shaken," replied Tim, "but other than that I'm OK."

"That was a fine bit of shooting," commented CAS. "I don't think I would have done any better myself."

Tim laughed.

"Coming from you, that's a big compliment," he said. "Now set course for the Command ship and get me out of here."

"Course set," confirmed CAS.

Home Again

As Tim flew back to the Command ship, he was flanked on one side by Red fighter I and on the other side by Red fighter III.

When they reached the hangar, the entire crew were there, standing in a guard of honour to meet them. Even Commander Ford and General Yore and General Lee had come down to the hangar.

Tim's fighter shuddered to a halt in its docking bay. He pulled back the cockpit cover and Uli helped him to climb out. Commander Ford immediately came over to shake his hand.

"Congratulations, Captain Tim," said the delighted Commander. "You have saved *Earth III*."

"Thank you, Commander," said Tim.

"Three cheers for Captain Tim!" shouted the Commander.

"Hip hip hooray," echoed around the hangar, three times.

"Now you must go immediately to the sick bay to have that injured arm looked at," said the Commander. "I will meet you on the Bridge after you have seen the doctor."

Uli showed Tim to the sick bay which was located close to the pilots' quarters.

The doctor was a small, pale man who wore a long white coat and small round glasses.

"That's a nasty laser burn you have there," he said, after he had examined Tim's injured arm.

From his coat pocket, he took out a small grey tube which contained an evil-smelling purple ointment. He smeared the ointment on Tim's shoulder and arm.

Tim gasped from shock as the freezing ointment hit his injured arm.

"That will take the sting out of the laser burn," said the doctor. "Your shoulder will be a bit stiff for a while, and you will have a red mark at the top of your arm, but it will pass."

The pain began to leave Tim's shoulder and arm at once and was replaced by a cold numbness.

"Thank you, doctor," he said.

When Tim and Uli reached the bridge, the Commander and the Generals were there waiting for them.

"How's your arm, Captain Tim?" asked the Commander.

"It's a bit stiff, but the pain is gone," Tim told him.

For the first time since Tim came on board the Commander looked happy, and the worried look had finally disappeared from his face.

"We have made contact with *Earth III*," he told Tim. "They ran out of fresh water a few demihours ago and were just about to surrender to the Rylons when you blew up the *Destroyer*. Needless to say, you are a hero on *Earth III*."

Being thought of as a hero made Tim feel embarrassed. He couldn't think of anything to say, so he stared shyly at the floor.

"We will be docking at *Earth III* shortly," continued the Commander. "There will be a big party tonight to celebrate the lifting of the siege and you, of course, will be the guest of honour."

"I'm afraid I'll have to miss the celebrations," said Tim. "It's time that I was getting back home."

The Commander looked disappointed, but he accepted Tim's decision.

"I won't try to change your mind," he said. "If you have to go, you have to go, but the least I can do is give you something to remember us by."

He reached into an inside pocket and took out a small silver medal with the picture of a fighter on it. He placed the medal in the palm of Tim's hand.

"This is our Medal of Courage," explained he Commander. "It is our highest honour and is only awarded for feats of great bravery. This particular medal was won by my grandfather a long time ago, and now I want you to have it."

Tim could see that the medal meant a lot to the Commander.

"I can't take that," he said humbly. "It belongs to you."

The Commander wouldn't hear of taking the medal back.

"I want you to have it," he insisted. "Never before have I seen such bravery. I have been holding on to that medal for a long time now, waiting to give it to someone worthy of it. Now at last I have found that person – I would be proud if you would accept the medal."

"Then I will be proud to have it," said Tim.

"Good," said the Commander. "Now we must get you to the transporter room before we dock at *Earth III*."

"My parents will be frantic with worry wondering what has happened to me," said Tim, as he the Commander and Uli walked towards the transportation room.

"You needn't worry about that," the Commander reassured him. "We are a parallel galaxy and the time here exists alongside other galaxies but independent of them.

"Although the time you have spent here was real while you were here, it will not be reflected in your world."

Tim thought for a moment before replying. "I don't think I really understand that," he admitted.

"What it means," explained the Commander, "is that very little time will have elapsed in your world."

"You mean I'll return at the same time I left," said Tim.

"Not exactly the same time," replied the Commander, "but very soon afterwards."

As Tim stepped into the glass transportation unit Commander Ford shook his hand warmly.

"On behalf of the whole Federation, I want to thank you again for all your help," he said.

"I was glad I was able to help," said Tim.

"Will we ever see you again?" asked Uli.

"That depends on the Commander," said Tim, glancing over at him.

"May I call you again if we need you?" asked the Commander.

"Of course you can," said Tim. "Any time."

Uli smiled, then closed the door of the transportation unit.

Inside the unit, it was completely silent and the glass sides felt cold. Tim could see the Commander's mouth moving as he said something to Uli, but he couldn't hear what was said.

Uli then went over to the control panel and pressed a few buttons.

Suddenly a circle of light moved up from the floor and began to spin slowly around Tim's feet. Gradually it picked up speed, until it was whizzing around his ankles. The circle moved higher and higher up his body, as more and more circles appeared. Up to his knees, then up his legs to his hips, and still the circles kept swirling and climbing.

A zinging noise started very quietly and echoed softly inside his head. The circles kept coming and moving higher and higher, up to his stomach and then his chest. The faces of the Commander and Uli shimmered and then faded, as if they had been swallowed up in a thick mist.

The circles climbed higher and higher and became tighter and tighter. They were now swirling around Tim's head. His gaze was drawn to a very bright dot that kept spinning in front of his eyes. He tried to look away, but he couldn't. He felt paralysed. His arms and legs wouldn't move. Then he was lifted off the floor and felt as if he was being sucked backwards down a long dark corridor. The faces of Commander Ford and Uli disappeared completely. The zinging noise got louder and louder, until it was ringing in his ears. Tim squeezed his Medal of Courage tightly and closed his eyes.

Gradually the zinging died away and the grip of the swirling circles slackened, until finally the sensation of movement had completely gone. Tim could no longer feel the cold glass of the transportation unit instead, something soft and warm pressed against his body.

Far in the distance, somebody was calling his name, over and over again. The voice came closer and closer, until it seemed to be right beside him.

"Tim!" called the voice. "Tim!"

Slowly, Tim opened one eye and then the other. A woman, who looked just like his mother, was looking down at him.

Gradually, Tim's consciousness returned. It *was* Mum and, what's more, he was lying in his own bed in his own room wearing his pyjamas.

"It's time to get up, Tim," said his mother again. "You'll be late for school."

How did I get here? he wondered. Was it all a dream?

His mother left the bedroom and Tim sat up straight in bed and pulled off his pyjama top. He examined his arm where he had been burnt by the Rylon laser. The red mark had disappeared. His shoulder did feel a little stiff, but that could be from lying on it all night.

He glanced over at his computer. The switch on the

wall was turned off, as he always left it when he was going to bed.

Tim was confused. It had all seemed so real, he thought . . . Uli, CAS, the Commander, *Alpha I* and the Rylons, but it had only been a dream.

"Get up, Tim," his mother shouted from downstairs.

Tim pulled back the bedcovers and jumped out of bed. A small silver object fell to the floor and landed beside his feet. He bent down and picked it up. It was a medal, a medal with a picture of a fighter on it. It was the Medal of Courage which Commander Ford had given him.

Suddenly, the computer bleeped and flashed. A message shot across the screen and then disappeared, but it had remained on the screen just long enough for Tim to read it:

"Thanks for your help. Commander Ford."

Tim smiled.

"So it wasn't a dream," he said to himself as he clutched the medal tightly. "It was real – it all really happened."

"Hurry up, Tim," shouted his mother, but Tim wasn't listening. He was miles away – millions of miles away in a parallel galaxy. He was thinking about what the Commander had said to him as he was leaving *Alpha I*: "May I call you again if we need you?"

Tim wondered just when the Commander might send for him again.